The Gallows Witness and Other Stories

by David Ray Foster

Cover design created by Strange Moon Press LLC.
Cat image sourced from public domain via Library of Congress.
www.loc.gov

Title font "Mirage Gothic" designed by Carlos Mario Peña Solís.

Strange Moon Press LLC
10 Benning St., Ste 160-168
West Lebanon, NH 03784
www.strangemoonpress.com

The Stories

The Gallows Witness

The cat remembered fire before it remembered flesh. It remembered the scent of tallow candles melting in damp air. It remembered the crackle of green wood refusing to burn cleanly. It remembered voices — hundreds of them — pressed tight with fear and righteousness. And it remembered her.

In 1692, the town of Salem was smaller than a modern parking lot. The roads were mud-rutted veins cutting between timber houses and fields half-harvested. The sky felt close then, low and gray as though listening. People prayed loudly in those days. They feared quietly.

On a March morning cold enough to split knuckles, they brought Sarah Greene to the meeting house in chains. She was not what they had expected a witch to be. She was neither bent nor shriveled. She did not spit curses or foam at the mouth. She was thirty-four years old, dark-haired, sharp-eyed, and calm. Too calm. The girls had screamed at her presence. Claimed her specter pinched them, choked them, whispered wicked promises in the night. Sarah had simply watched. Beside her — though only some claimed to see it — a black cat with pale, reflective eyes

Judge Nathaniel Harwood presided that day. He was a man who believed certainty was holiness. He believed doubt was a crack through which Satan entered. When Sarah was asked to confess, she did not. When pressed to name accomplices, she did not. When warned that refusal would condemn her, she said quietly, "Truth will not be frightened into lying."

The room shifted then. Murmurs. Gasps. Judge Harwood leaned forward. "You consort with a familiar spirit," he said.

Sarah tilted her head slightly. "And you consort with fear," a response that sealed her fate.

They hanged her on Gallows Hill.

The sky was the color of iron. The rope creaked once before tightening. The crowd watched. Some prayed. Some wept. Some smiled thinly. Judge Harwood did not look away. As Sarah stood on the ladder, her hands bound, she searched the crowd. Her gaze did not find mercy. It found the cat.

The cat sat upon a boulder at the edge of the clearing. Black fur absorbing light. Eyes like pale moons. No one else seemed to notice it. Sarah smiled faintly. When the rope snapped tight, and the air left her body, the cat did not flinch. It only blinked. Once.

That night, Judge Harwood dreamed. He walked alone through the woods beyond town. The branches clawed at his coat. Snow fell, though it had not snowed in waking life. Ahead, something moved. Low. Silent. The black cat stepped into view. Its eyes gleamed pale as bone. "I have done God's will," Harwood muttered in his dream. The cat opened its mouth. Its jaw split wider than the bone allows. Inside was not flesh, but darkness.

From that darkness came Sarah's voice: "You have done your own will." Harwood awoke choking.

Within a year, two of his children would die of sudden fever. His wife would waste slowly, claiming she heard scratching beneath the floorboards. Harwood himself would die in winter, alone, raving of silver eyes watching from corners. The town called it God's mysterious will. The cat called it memory. Centuries passed.

Salem changed. The mud roads became pavement. The meeting house became a museum. Tourists came each October to buy witch hats and cinnamon-scented candles. They posed for photographs near plaques commemorating the trials. Few remembered names. Few understood the weight of fear that once hung like smoke. But some bloodlines endure. And memory can follow blood.

In modern Salem, the Harwood name still carried quiet prestige. The judge's great-great-great-great-grandson — Daniel Harwood — lived in a restored colonial home three streets from the old trial site. He was forty-two. A criminal defense attorney, well respected, measured, logical. He did not believe in curses. He did not believe in ghosts. He believed in precedent. He liked to remind dinner guests that the trials were a "complex sociopolitical event." He disliked it when people romanticized witches. "They weren't witches," he would say with a polite smile. "They were victims of mass hysteria."

He did not speak often of his ancestor. But he kept the old journals, leather-bound, faded ink. They were locked in a display cabinet in his study.

The cat appeared on an October evening.

Tourist season. The air smelled of kettle corn and fallen leaves. Daniel was pouring himself a glass of wine when he noticed something through the study window.

On the low stone wall bordering his yard sat a black cat. It was too dark to see clearly. But its eyes—Even from inside the house, seemed pale, reflective.

He frowned. Strays were common this time of year. He stepped outside. The cat did not run. It watched him approach. Its fur was unnaturally sleek. No burrs. No dirt. No collar. Its eyes were not green. Not gold. They were gray-white, like old bone. Daniel felt something then — faint, like pressure behind the bridge of his nose. "Shoo," he said. The cat blinked. It did not move. "Go on." He stepped closer.

For a fraction of a second — less than a blink — he thought he saw something else behind the eyes. Not reflection, depth, as though the pupils were openings into a space far larger than the body containing them. He stepped back involuntarily. The cat turned its head slowly toward the house, then back at him. It leapt lightly from the wall and disappeared into shadow. Daniel told himself it was nothing.

That night, he dreamed of rope, not the abstract idea of it, the sensation. Fibers are tightening against skin. He felt cold air on his face. Heard distant murmuring. He tried to move but could not. Across from him stood a woman. Her dark hair loose over her shoulders, eyes steady. "You judge without knowing," she said.

He awoke with a start. The digital clock glowed 3:17 a.m. From downstairs came a sound. A soft scratch. Daniel sat upright. The scratch came again, from the study. He rose slowly and descended the stairs. The house felt colder than it should. The thermostat read seventy-two. The study door stood slightly ajar. He did not remember leaving it that way. He pushed it open.

The display cabinet stood against the far wall, unlocked. The journal from 1692 lay open on the desk. Daniel was certain he had not removed it. His pulse quickened. A shadow moved near the window. The cat sat on the sill. Inside. It must have slipped through an open vent or chimney. Its pale eyes fixed on him. Daniel swallowed. "Get out." The cat did not respond. Instead, it lifted one paw and placed it deliberately on the open journal.

The page beneath bore his ancestor's handwriting. A passage he had read before but never truly considered.

She does not tremble. It unsettles the girls. I feel in her gaze an unspoken accusation. I will see her hanged.

The ink looked darker tonight…..Wet.

Daniel took a step forward. The cat's pupils widened. For a moment, the room seemed to stretch. The walls are bending subtly outward. The temperature dropped sharply. Frost formed along the windowpane. Daniel blinked hard. The cat was gone. The room returned to normal. The journal lay closed, the locked cabinet untouched. He stood alone. Breathing hard.

In the following days, Daniel dismissed the incident as stress. He had a difficult case pending. A man is accused of assaulting his stepdaughter. The evidence was murky. The girl's testimony is inconsistent. Daniel believed in due process, believed in dismantling weak arguments. He had built a career on it. Still, he could not ignore the unease.

On his walk to work one morning, he saw the cat again. It sat outside the courthouse. Among tourists. No one else seemed to notice it. Its pale eyes tracked him. He hesitated. The sensation returned — pressure behind his brow. This time it came with something else. A whisper. Not audible, but unmistakable. Memory. He saw a rope. He saw Sarah's calm face. He saw his ancestor's steady hand signing a death warrant.

He stumbled slightly. A passerby asked if he was all right.

"Yes," he muttered, but he was not.

The dreams grew clearer, not abstract. Specific. He stood not as himself, but as Judge Harwood. He felt the weight of the wool coat. The scratch of lace at his throat. He heard Sarah's voice — calm, measured. "You mistake fear for righteousness." He felt the satisfaction of condemnation. The certainty. The pride. And then—the rope. This time it was around his own neck. He awoke gasping, hands at his throat.

In the corner of his bedroom, two pale eyes watched. The cat sat atop his dresser. It had not made a sound entering.

"How are you here?" Daniel whispered. The cat stepped down lightly, its body seemed longer than before, its tail is too fluid. It moved toward him. Each step is soundless. When it reached the foot of the bed, it sat. And stared. Daniel's breath came shallow. "What do you want?" The cat's head tilted slightly, in that moment, he knew. It did not want. It remembered. And memory had chosen him.

Across town, a plaque marked the approximate site of Gallows Hill. Tourists posed for photographs. Children ran laughing across the grass that once held fear. That evening, as twilight fell, a black cat appeared atop the plaque. Its eyes shone pale in the dim light. A wind rose unexpectedly. Leaves skittered across stone. The cat lifted its head. And for the first time in three centuries—It felt the line of blood draw taut.

Daniel Harwood stood at his study window miles away, watching darkness gather. Behind him, the journal from 1692 lay open again.

Though he had locked it and written in the margin, in ink not yet dry—A single line:

"The rope remembers the hand that knots it."

Daniel's reflection in the glass did not move when he did, it stood still, eyes pale, almost silver.

Daniel did not remember picking up the pen, yet there it was — black ink still wet along the margin of his ancestor's journal. "The rope remembers the hand that knots it."

Outside, wind pressed against the glass. A thin branch scraped across the pane with a dry, deliberate sound. Scratch. Scratch. He turned slowly. The yard was empty. No cat. No movement. But the air inside the study felt altered — thinner, as if the room were only pretending to hold oxygen. Daniel closed the journal carefully and locked the cabinet again. He tugged the handle twice to be certain. Then he went upstairs, leaving the lights on below. He did not want darkness gathering unobserved.

The next morning, he arrived at court exhausted.

The case of *Commonwealth v. Rowan Pike* was scheduled for motion arguments. Pike was accused of assaulting his fourteen-year-old stepdaughter. Daniel's role was clear: challenge the admissibility of testimony, dissect inconsistencies, and ensure the burden of proof remained heavy. He had done it before. Many times. He had told himself it was a principle.

Justice requires balance. Emotion clouds facts.

As he stood in the courtroom — polished wood, fluorescent hum — he felt the pressure again between his brows. He glanced toward the gallery. In the back row, unnoticed by others, sat the black cat. Perfectly still. Silver-pale eyes fixed on him. His throat tightened. He blinked. The seat was empty. He told himself it was a lack of sleep.

When the girl took the stand, Daniel's voice felt unfamiliar to him — too sharp, too clinical. "You previously stated the incident occurred in May," he said evenly. "Yet today you've said April. Which is it?"

The girl faltered. Daniel pressed. Procedure. Precision. But with each question, he heard something layered beneath his own voice. Another cadence. Older. "You consort with fear." He faltered mid-sentence.

For a moment, the courtroom blurred. In its place stood a timbered meeting house. Candles flickered.

A rope hung visible through an open door, and on the bench across from him stood Sarah Greene. Not bruised. Not broken. Calm. "You judge without knowing," she said softly. The image vanished. Daniel realized the courtroom had fallen silent. The judge stared at him. "Mr. Harwood?"

He swallowed. "My apologies, Your Honor." He finished the cross-examination more gently than planned. When he stepped outside afterward, the sky above Salem had turned prematurely gray. At the base of the courthouse steps sat the cat. Waiting.

That night, Daniel did not lock the study. He left the journal on the desk intentionally. He poured himself a drink and sat across from it. "If this is some kind of psychological break," he muttered, "let's have it done."

The house creaked. Minutes passed. Then the temperature shifted — subtle but undeniable. A current of cold brushed his ankles. He did not look toward the window. He did not need to. He felt it enter. A soft thud on hardwood. Claws clicking once. Twice. The cat stepped into view.

Its fur seemed darker tonight — less like black and more like absence. Its eyes reflected the lamplight as pale disks. Daniel did not stand. "You think I am him," he said quietly. The cat blinked. "You think blood is guilt." Silence. Its tail curled neatly around its paws.

Daniel leaned forward. "I am not Judge Nathaniel Harwood. I did not sign death warrants. I did not hang women." The cat's head tilted slightly. The pressure behind his brow intensified. Memory flooded him — not his own. A ladder on Gallows Hill. The roughness of rope fibers against skin. A crowd's murmuring hunger. His ancestor's face — composed, righteous. Then, another memory.

Judge Harwood at his desk, years later. Alone. Hearing scratching beneath the floorboards. Calling for servants who did not answer. Seeing pale eyes at the foot of his bed. The cat rose. It walked toward him. With each step, its body elongated subtly. The spine arches higher. The legs are thinning. The shadow beneath it was widening like spilled ink.

Daniel's pulse hammered. "I am not him," he repeated, though the certainty in his voice thinned. The cat stopped a few feet away. Its mouth opened. Not in a hiss, something else. The jaw parted too far. too wide. Darkness filled the opening, from that darkness came Sarah's voice. "Blood remembers." Daniel's chair scraped as he pushed back. "What do you want from me?" The layered answer came like wind through a graveyard. "Balance." The cat's form stretched further.

The rib cage split open like a charred door. Inside the hollow cavity, shapes pressed outward. Not only Sarah, but others. Bridget. Martha. Rebecca.

Women condemned.

Their faces not decayed—etched in memory. Daniel staggered backward. "This isn't justice," he whispered. "This is vengeance."

The silver eyes flared brighter. "You speak as he did."

The temperature plummeted, frost crawled along the edges of the journal pages. Daniel's breath fogged the air. He felt the rope then — phantom-tight around his throat. He clawed at nothing. The cat stepped closer. Inside its chest cavity, Sarah's face moved forward. Calm as ever. "You defend harm," she said softly. Daniel shook his head violently. "I defend the law." "You defend power." The word struck like a bell.

Images crashed into him — Rowan Pike's stepdaughter shrinking under cross-examination. Other cases. Other clients. Men who had walked free because doubt was expertly carved. Had he known? Had he suspected? He had told himself it was not his role to know. The rope tightened. His knees buckled. The cat loomed above him now, no longer feline but something tall and wrong, composed of shadow and bone-light.

The woman stepped partially from its hollow chest, not solid but present.

"You are not him," Sarah said. Daniel gasped. "Then why—" " You carry him." The rope slackened slightly. "You may choose differently."

The cat's silver gaze pierced him. Daniel understood then — not as words, but as weight. This was not execution. Not yet.

This was reckoning.

The creature did not kill indiscriminately. It corrected. It hollowed those who refused. His ancestor had refused and had been emptied. Daniel's throat burned. "What happens if I refuse?" he rasped. The cat's mouth closed. The darkness within sealed. The silver eyes dimmed slightly. "You have seen." It was enough of an answer.

The next morning, Daniel withdrew from Rowan Pike's defense. Officially citing "conflict of conscience." The legal community buzzed with speculation. He did not elaborate. That evening, he visited the trial memorial site near Gallows Hill. The air was crisp. Tourists had thinned. He stood before the stone markers bearing the names of the condemned. He read each one aloud. Slowly.

The wind stirred as he spoke Sarah Greene's name. Behind him, paws touched grass. He did not turn immediately. When he did, the cat sat a few yards away. Small again. Contained. Silver eyes reflecting twilight. Daniel exhaled shakily. "I cannot undo what he did," he said. The cat blinked. "I cannot erase blood." The cat's head tilted. "But I can refuse to tighten the rope." Silence stretched between them.

The wind quieted. The cat rose. It walked toward the stones.

For a moment, as it passed before Sarah's marker, its body shimmered — elongating, thinning — then settling back into feline form. Daniel felt the pressure behind his brow ease for the first time. Not vanish. But soften. The cat turned to him one final time. Its silver eyes held no rage now. Only measure. Then it stepped into shadow. And was gone.

Weeks passed.

Daniel changed firms. He shifted his practice to advocacy work — representing minors in protective custody hearings, assisting victims rather than dismantling them. It did not erase his past cases. It did not absolve lineage. But it altered the trajectory. Sometimes, late at night, he would sense it still. A presence on the periphery.

Not threatening.

Watching. Weighing.

On the anniversary of Sarah Greene's execution, Daniel returned to Gallows Hill. He brought flowers. He knelt by the marker. "Balance," he murmured. Behind him, soft paws brushed stone. He did not look. He did not need to. The cat sat in the fading light. Black fur absorbing dusk. Silver eyes pale and steady.

It had waited three centuries for the line of blood to bend. It had not sought death. Only correction.

In 1692, fear had worn the mask of righteousness. In 2026, justice wore sharper suits. But memory endured. And so did the familiar. When the sun dipped below the horizon, the cat rose. Its form flickered briefly — taller, elongated, rib cage faintly aglow with remembered faces. Sarah's voice whispered once more into the wind. "Truth need not tremble." The shape folded inward, collapsing back into feline grace. Then it stepped into shadow.

Some say black cats bring misfortune. Others say they are omens. In Salem, if you walk near the old stones at twilight, you may glimpse pale eyes watching from the edge of the trees. They do not judge without knowing. They do not strike without memory. They wait, for bloodlines to choose, for ropes to be set down. for fear to loosen its grip.

When the balance tips—they rise. Not always to kill, but to always remember.

The Cat Who Remembered

Rain fell softly on the shingles of the old house nestled at the edge of the rocky coast. It was the kind of coastal rain that didn't lash or thunder but whispered against the windows, a constant hush that seemed to soothe more than startle.

Michael Bell sat alone in his study, surrounded by books that hadn't been opened in years. The fire had burned down to a dull glow, and he could hear the sigh of wind pressing faintly against the windowpanes.

He was seventy-six years old and had lived in that house alone for the past twenty-three of them. Widowed young, with no children and few friends still breathing, Michael had carved out a quiet existence as the village's old librarian, now retired. The townsfolk respected him, even liked him, but they never truly knew him. They couldn't see the ghosts that lingered in his eyes, or the ache that still stirred in his chest when certain songs played or the sea smelled a particular way.

That night, as Michael prepared to douse the fire and make his way to bed, he heard the sound. It was soft, so soft he wasn't sure it was real at first. A thud. A scratch. A pause. Then again — scratch-scratch. Not frantic, but deliberate.

He turned from the hearth, blinking. He was not a man prone to fancy, but the sound was unmistakably at his front door. He waited, half expecting the sound to vanish as easily as it came. It did not. Grumbling under his breath, Arthur retrieved his robe, lit the hall lamp, and shuffled to the front door.

When he opened it, the wind carried in the smell of salt and pine. Rain painted the porch in glimmering black streaks. And at the threshold, huddled against the cold, sat a cat.

It was a tabby, though its coat shimmered oddly in the lamplight, almost silver in the rain. Its green eyes met his with an unsettling calm, as though it had been waiting for him. "Well," Michael muttered, "you've got nerve." The cat blinked, unbothered.

He should have shut the door.

Should have left it to the night and the wild. But something in him, some thread woven from memory and loneliness, bent toward mercy. Michael opened the door wider. "Come on, then."

The cat padded in without hesitation.

The next morning dawned in streaks of pewter and rose, soft light diffusing through gauzy curtains. Arthur stirred in bed, startled to feel warmth not from the electric blanket, but from a small, breathing bundle curled near his feet, the cat.

He sat up slowly, rubbing sleep from his eyes. The feline stretched luxuriously, then hopped down with practiced grace, tail curling like a question mark as it trotted toward the kitchen.

"I suppose you think you live here now," Michael said aloud, voice gruff with sleep. He stood and winced at the ache in his joints. "We'll see about that."

In the kitchen, the cat sat beside the cupboard, as if it knew exactly where the cans of sardines were stored. Michael opened a tin and set it down on a saucer. The cat sniffed, then ate daintily, its manners oddly refined.

After breakfast, Michael settled into his old armchair with a copy of The Wind in the Willows but found himself distracted. The cat had disappeared somewhere into the house. He didn't hear it move, yet every so often, he'd glimpse a flick of its silver tail rounding a corner. It was uncanny.

That night, the strangeness began.

Michael lit the fireplace as he did every evening. When he knelt to prod the embers, he noticed something glinting in the ashes. Curious, he reached in with the poker and drew out a small object. It was an old key — tarnished bronze with an ornate bow. He didn't remember ever owning such a key.

Holding it up to the light, Michael turned it over in his hand. Something about it stirred the dust in his memory. The cat appeared beside him then, silently. Its green eyes flicked from the key to his face. Michael laughed nervously. "What, you trying to show me something?"

The cat blinked.

Later that night, after a fitful sleep, Michael dreamed of Margaret. They were young again, sitting in the garden behind his father's old house. She was laughing, her red scarf blowing in the wind. The lilacs were in bloom. But just as he reached for her hand, the scene changed. She was walking away, suitcase in hand, and he stood at the train station unable to move. When he awoke, he felt tears drying on his cheeks.

The cat sat on the windowsill, silhouetted against the gray light. Watching.

The key burned a hole in his pocket all morning. Michael tried to ignore it, tried to busy himself with the small rituals of solitude—watering the single fern in the parlor, sweeping the front steps, feeding the cat (who now answered, when it chose to, to the name "Thistle.")

But the key called to him, and by noon, he gave in.

The attic door was old and seldom opened. It creaked on its hinges like a ship's hull groaning in deep water. Dust motes danced in the thin sunlight as he climbed the stairs, flashlight in hand, Thistle close behind. There, tucked behind an old trunk filled with winter quilts, was a wooden box bound with a lock. The key slid in smoothly.

Inside were letters. Dozens of them, yellowed with age, tied in a red ribbon now faded to pink. Arthur's breath caught in his throat. He recognized the handwriting immediately — his own. These were the letters he had written to Margaret after she left. Letters he never sent. Letters he had forgotten.

They were filled with longing, regret, and flashes of bitter anger softened by sorrow. One line stood out: "If you ever return, I will be waiting. Even if the sea turns to stone, I will be here." Thistle sat beside him, tail wrapped around its paws, silent as a priest.

That night, the wind carried the scent of lilacs through the house though none were in bloom.

Micheal began walking the cliffs again. It had once been a daily ritual, long before his knees turned traitor and solitude settled in like ivy on stone. But now, each morning after breakfast — shared with Thistle, who now followed him like a shadow — he bundled himself in his thick wool coat and took to the sea path.

It was on the fourth morning that he saw her. A woman in a long gray coat, standing at the far end of the rocky overlook, hair pale and loose in the wind. She was turned away from him, staring out over the surf. Something in the curve of her shoulders made Michael's breath catch.

He called out, but the wind snatched the word away.

By the time he reached the spot, she was gone. Over the next few days, he saw her again. Always at a distance. Always silent. But never quite gone.

One morning, he brought a sketchbook and tried to draw her face from memory. The pencil in his hand moved with unexpected ease. When he looked down at the page, his heart pounded — it was Margaret's face, just as she had been thirty years ago.

That night, Michael did not dream. Instead, he awoke at 3:17 a.m., the room awash in moonlight. Thistle was on his chest, staring directly into his eyes. And somewhere in the house, an old phonograph played a lilting tune they had once danced to.

Two days after the last sighting of the woman, Michael found something peculiar in the mail. He rarely received anything beyond the occasional catalog or the monthly statement from the local bank. But this was different—a small cream-colored envelope, sealed with a red wax stamp bearing an unfamiliar crest. No return address. No postage. Just his name: Michael Bell, written in handwriting so precise it felt more calligraphy than ink.

His fingers trembled slightly as he opened it. Inside was a single piece of paper. It read "You once promised you'd wait. I never stopped hearing your words." No signature. But he didn't need one. Margaret. Michael sat down heavily in his kitchen chair. Thistle leapt up beside him, as if he too had been expecting this. "Am I losing it?" Michael muttered.

Thistle only stared.

That night, he took out the letters again and reread them all. Every word was an echo. Every sentence a plea. And when he was done, he laid them beside the mysterious note, forming a bridge across time. He didn't know what was happening. Only that the air had shifted — as if the past was beginning to fold back into the present.

The cat, ever silent, remained by his side.

Michael hadn't stepped foot in the village historical society in over a decade. The building was squat and square, with yellowed windows and a peeling sign that read Alder Bay Archives. Inside, it smelled of dust and old paper. The curator was still Mrs. Dobbins, a formidable woman with steel-gray hair and a stare that could melt glass. She seemed surprised to see him.

"Michael Bell," she said. "Come back from the grave, have you?"

"Not yet," Michael replied, managing a tired smile. "I'm looking for someone. A woman who used to live here… or maybe passed through." He gave Margaret's full name.

Dobbins narrowed her eyes. "Margaret Winters," she said. "Now there's a name I haven't heard in a long time."

She disappeared into a back room and returned with a slim file, tied with a faded ribbon. Inside were a few clippings — a wedding announcement from 1971, a police report from 1980 about a missing woman, and a final document: a change-of-name record dated 1993.

It showed that Margaret Winters had taken a new identity and moved to Vermont.

Michael's hand trembled. There was also a recent note scribbled on the back of one form: Saw her once at the florist's on Miller Street. Same lilacs in her hair. Looked right at me. Didn't say a word. "Miller Street," Michael whispered.

Thistle, waiting patiently by the door, flicked his tail once. A direction, a sign.

Michael packed a small overnight bag. Just enough for a few days, though he had no idea how long he might be gone. As he zipped it closed, Thistle jumped onto the bed and stared at him with a quiet insistence. There was no question now—the cat was coming, too. They left at dawn.

The drive to Vermont took nearly six hours. Michael stopped twice, once for gas and once to let Thistle out to stretch. To his surprise, the cat walked calmly beside him at a rest stop, then hopped back into the car as if it were the most natural thing in the world.

By late afternoon, they arrived in a town called Hollowford. It was small, picturesque, with a single main street lined by old clapboard buildings and a town green that looked like it hadn't changed since the 1950s.

Michael asked a gas station attendant where Miller Street

was. The boy pointed north. "It's near the river. Kinda tucked back. There's a florist shop down there. Real pretty place."

The shop was called The Green Stem. Its windows were full of cascading ivy and pots of fresh lilacs

Michael's heart began to hammer. He didn't go in. Not yet. He sat on a bench across the street, watching. For a long time, nothing happened. Then she stepped outside. Margaret. Older, slower, her once auburn hair now silvered, swept into a bun. But it was her. Every line of her face, every motion of her hands as she adjusted a pot near the door.

Michael couldn't breathe. Thistle sat beside him, tail flicking, eyes narrowed. "I can't," Michael whispered. "What if she doesn't remember me?" Thistle stood and jumped down, walked across the street and waited at the door of the shop.

The bell above the door jingled as Michael stepped into the shop. The air smelled of lilacs and rose water and something else—warm earth, perhaps, or memory. Margaret was behind the counter, arranging white roses. She looked up.

Their eyes met.

For a moment, time unraveled. There was no florist's shop, no thirty years, no sorrow.

Just Michael and Margaret, as they had once been. She spoke first. "I was wondering when you'd come."

Michael's voice cracked. "You knew?"

"I saw the cat." She nodded toward Thistle, who sat regally in the doorway. "He comes before the past does."

He crossed the room slowly, tears in his eyes. "I thought you were gone forever."

"I thought you'd forgotten me."

"I never did. I waited. I wrote to you. I didn't send them, but—"

"I know. I heard them."

She stepped out from behind the counter. They stood face to face, older, wiser, wounded by time but not broken. Margaret took his hand. "I always hoped you'd find me." Michael squeezed her fingers. "You were never lost."

Outside, the sun began to sink. Thistle turned his gaze to the west, where the light burned gold and orange on the horizon.

Margaret brought Michael back to a small white house nestled behind a row of pines on Ellery Lane. It was quiet and overgrown, with a gate that squeaked and windows that still wore lace curtains. "I bought it after I changed my name," she explained as she unlocked the door.

"I needed somewhere the past couldn't follow. Somewhere I could learn how to live again."

Michael stepped inside. The air was warm, filled with the scent of lavender and old wood. Photographs lined the mantel — a life rebuilt, solitary but soft. There were no pictures of him, of them, but he felt their absence keenly.

She made tea while he sat in the armchair by the fireplace. Thistle prowled the perimeter of the room, pausing once beneath a window to stare out into the dusk.

"You should be angry," she said as she handed him a cup.

"I was," Michael replied. "For years. Then I buried it. Now I think I'm just… grateful. To see you again."

Margaret smiled. "You were always too gentle."

They sat in silence, sipping tea and letting the decades peel away like bark from a tree. As the evening wore on, they moved to the sofa, and Margaret retrieved an old music box. When she wound it, it played their song — the one from the phonograph, the one Thistle had summoned.

Michael laughed softly. "You kept it."

"I never could throw it away."

Outside, the moon climbed high. And for the first time in thirty years, Arthur and Margaret sat beside each other, not as ghosts but as something whole. They stayed in Hollowford for a week.

Michael extended his visit each morning without saying why, and Margaret never asked. It was as though they both understood the fragile beauty of what they had — a rare second chance, borrowed time beneath golden leaves.

They walked the river path hand in hand. They cooked small meals. They laughed. They forgave.

Thistle watched it all with serene approval.

On the seventh night, they returned from a walk to find the lilac bushes around Margaret's porch in full bloom — though the season had long since passed.

Michael and Margaret sat together on the porch swing as the stars blinked into being.

"You know," Michael said, "when I first saw that cat, I thought he was just lost. But I think he found me instead."

"He did," Margaret whispered. "He brought you back."

Thistle climbed onto the porch rail, tail swishing. He looked between them one last time.

Then, without a sound, he stood. His outline began to shimmer, as if touched by dew or moonlight. And before their eyes, Thistle began to fade. First his tail, then his limbs, until only his eyes remained — two green sparks in the night.

And then those too vanished.

On the porch floor where he had last sat, a single lilac pet-
al drifted down. Michael reached for Margaret's hand.
She took it. They sat in silence for a long time, hearts full,
tears gentle.

Together again.

At last.

The Cat on Route 76

PART ONE: The Scenic Route

The interstate was a straight line of brake lights and anger, and Greg McAllister had had enough.

They'd been crawling through bumper-to-bumper traffic for over two hours somewhere outside of Roanoke, and the heat was melting tempers faster than popsicles in a July sun.

"Google says there's a back road that'll shave off an hour," Greg muttered, squinting at the screen of his phone.

Karen, riding shotgun with her sunglasses perched on her head and a scowl beginning to bloom, didn't look up. "It also says that road hasn't been updated since 2014. There are probably potholes big enough to eat the car."

Greg smiled anyway, the kind of tired, optimistic grin that had gotten him through twelve years of marriage, two kids, and a soul-sucking job in logistics. "Come on, hon. Let's make it an adventure."

In the backseat, Noah, twelve, and Emma, nine, were already arguing over whose turn it was to pick the next playlist. A half-eaten bag of pretzels lay open between them, and a juice box had been knocked over without comment.

"I swear to God, if you two keep fighting, we're turning around and going back to New Jersey!" Karen snapped.

Emma slumped back dramatically, arms crossed. "You always take his side."

Greg sighed and took the next exit. The back road—Route 76, according to the faded sign—was narrow, winding, and lined with ancient trees that pressed in like silent sentinels. The air felt heavier somehow. The sun had slipped behind the mountains, and twilight settled like a fog.

The kids' bickering faded as the scenery changed. Cell signals dropped to nothing. The playlist stopped. The silence that replaced it was a little too thick, too full of expectation.

Then Emma sat up straight. "Daddy, there's a kitty!"

Greg hit the brakes.

A black cat stood squarely in the middle of the road, perfectly still, its silhouette framed against the dying light. Its eyes glowed faintly green.

Karen leaned forward. "Is it… staring at us?"

Greg honked. The cat didn't move.

"Maybe it's hurt," Emma said, unbuckling her seatbelt.

"Stay in the car," Karen and Greg said in unison.

Then, just as suddenly as it appeared, the cat turned its head toward the woods, then vanished into the underbrush.

"Creepy," Noah muttered.

Karen turned toward Greg. "Maybe we should turn around."

Greg shook his head. "Just a cat."

But he was already checking the rearview mirror more often than usual.

PART TWO: Burrow County

They passed a rotted wooden sign not long after that:

WELCOME TO BURROW COUNTY — POP. ??

"Population unknown?" Karen said aloud, unease creeping into her voice. "What is this place?"

another car in over an hour. And then it happened again.

The cat.

Same coal-black fur. Same burning green eyes.

It sat at the edge of the road this time, tail flicking slowly. Watching…Always watching.

Greg slowed but didn't stop. "That is the same damn cat."

"Did we circle back somehow?" Karen asked.

"No way. I've been following the road."

Emma whispered, "I think he's warning us."

Karen turned fully in her seat. "Sweetie, it's just—"

Then they saw the sign: GAS • SNACKS • AIR.

Greg veered toward the gravel lot. The gas station ahead looked abandoned. No lights. No movement. The windows were boarded. An ancient pump leaned sideways on its rusted base.

And sitting on the pump was the cat.

PART THREE: Thistle Fork

The gas station was barely standing. One flick of wind and it'd fold in on itself like a house of cards. Greg pulled the SUV alongside the leaning pump, his fingers tightening around the steering wheel.

"No way this place works," Karen muttered.

"Tank's half full. Just stopping to check the map," Greg said, though he didn't believe it himself.

The cat watched from the top of the pump, tail curled neatly around its paws. It blinked—once—and then turned its head toward the woods again.

Always toward the woods, Greg thought. His stomach coiled.

"I'm staying in the car," Karen said, folding her arms.

Greg stepped out into the humid stillness. The air smelled like wet rust and something else—meat, maybe, left too long in the sun. He approached the boarded-up windows. There was a faint sound from inside, like humming. Low.

Off-key. Wrong.

He peered through a crack.

A man stood just beyond the boards, eyes wide open, staring at the door. His mouth moved like he was chewing something but never swallowing. His hands twitched at his sides. He didn't blink.

Greg staggered back. The humming stopped. When he looked again, the man was gone.

The cat meowed, sharp and urgent. It jumped off the pump and trotted toward the tree line.

Greg turned back to the SUV. "We're not staying here."

Karen was already shaking her head. "No arguments from me."

They drove. Fast.

The road twisted like intestines. At some point, the asphalt vanished and became dirt. They passed a burned-out barn. Then a gutted sedan, covered in moss and vines. No signs of life.

"I want to go home," Emma whispered.

Karen reached back, trying to comfort her. "It's going to be okay."
But even she didn't believe it.

They passed a road sign with no writing—just a single symbol etched into the rusted metal: a crude drawing of a cat with Xs for eyes.

Then Emma screamed.

"The cat! Again!"

It stood in the center of the road, unmoving.

Greg stopped just in time.

And just ahead—half-hidden in the trees—they saw movement.

Five… maybe six figures. Standing still. Watching. Some held tools. One had what looked like a bloody axe. Another held a bone, sharpened into a blade.

Karen clapped her hand over her mouth. Noah slid down in his seat.

The cat hissed. Loud. Unnatural. A rumble more than a meow.

The figures stopped. Then retreated into the woods, melting into shadow.

Greg didn't wait. He floored it.

The cat vanished into the trees.

PART FOUR: The Thing in the Night

They didn't make it out that night. The road became a path, and the path gave up entirely. Branches closed in above them. Greg finally stopped at a clearing surrounded by a fence of dead trees.

"I don't think we're going to find our way until morning," he said, voice thin.

Karen was pale. "We'll take turns sleeping."

They pitched the tent. Emma and Noah refused to sleep alone. The air was thick with insects. The moon rose late and blood-red.

Greg's flashlight barely worked.

And then, sometime around 3 a.m., Greg heard it.

Scrape. Drag. Sniff. Shuffle.

Outside the tent.

A sound like something pulling itself along the dirt. Claws on dry earth. Breathing—wet and ragged.

Greg held his breath. Karen clutched his hand, nails biting into skin.

Then—something pushed against the tent wall.

A hand.

Five fingers. Long. Wrong
.
It traced the shape of Emma's body from outside the nylon fabric. Slowly. Caressingly.

Greg moved.

The figure shrieked—high and keening, a sound that didn't belong in the world—and the shape vanished.

They burst out of the tent with flashlights and a flare Greg kept for emergencies.

The clearing was empty.

But beside the car, the cat sat. Its eyes shone like headlights.

And just beyond it, in the grass—blood. A trail. Leading back into the trees.

PART FIVE: The Burrow Folk

Morning broke late, filtered through a sickly yellow haze. The woods around the clearing were silent—too silent. No birdsong.

No wind. Just heavy, listening quiet.

Greg didn't speak as he packed up the tent. He kept glancing over his shoulder, waiting for something to move in the trees. Karen helped, but her hands were shaking.

The children didn't complain. They'd seen the hand on the tent. They'd seen the blood trail.

They all saw the cat again too—this time sitting on the hood of the SUV, licking one paw slowly, as if last night hadn't happened.

"What is that thing?" Karen whispered.

Emma, her voice quiet and certain, said, "He's not a cat."

They tried to drive, but the road was gone. Literally gone—swallowed by mud and thick vines. They doubled back and tried another path. Same result. Greg swore under his breath, panic starting to creep into his words.

Then Noah shouted, "There's a house!"
At first, it looked abandoned—gray slats, a sagging porch, shutters hanging like broken limbs. But the chimney smoked faintly.

Greg didn't want to stop.

Karen said, "We don't have a choice."

They approached slowly. The cat darted ahead and sat on the porch, watching.

An old woman opened the door.

She wore a patchwork dress and a smile that didn't touch her eyes. Her face was leathery and slack, like it had melted in the sun and dried crooked.

"Well, bless your hearts," she crooned. "You folks look lost."

Inside, the house smelled like boiled roots and something metallic. Dried herbs hung from the ceiling, but some were clearly not herbs. Something dangled that looked suspiciously like a squirrel's paw… or a small human hand.

The old woman introduced herself as Gramma Netty. Her voice crackled like static.

She insisted they sit. Said she had stew on the stove. Karen tried to politely decline.

Netty smiled wider, revealing teeth like yellow needles.

Greg scanned the room. No phones. No clock. Just an old rifle on the mantle and a painting of a family—all of them looking slightly… off. Too many eyes. Faces too long. And then he saw the calendar. The year was 1992.

"Where are we, exactly?" Greg asked.

Netty stirred her pot and said, "You're in the holler. Burrow County. Not many find it 'less it's meant."

Outside, the cat sat still on the windowsill, tail flicking.

When Netty left the room to fetch something, Greg whispered, "We need to go. Now."

Karen nodded.

But the kids were staring at something under the couch. A trapdoor.

Nailed shut. Fresh blood on the woodgrain.

And then they heard it—a low, guttural moan from beneath the floorboards.

Netty's voice floated in from the kitchen. "Some don't die the first time. You got to soften the meat, 'fore you can use it right…"

Emma gasped.

That's when Netty screamed.

Not in fear. In fury.

The cat had jumped through the window, landed in the stew pot, and knocked it to the floor. Bones scattered—too long to be animal.

"WITCH-CAT!" Netty screeched, grabbing a cleaver.

Greg tackled her. "RUN!"

The family bolted through the door. Behind them, Gramma Netty wailed, "They're gettin' away! Call the BOYS!"

They didn't get far.

Just past the house, a wire stretched across the road. Greg didn't see it until it snapped up and slammed into the SUV's tires, shredding them. The car spun, crashed into a tree.

Smoke.

Screams.

Silence.

Greg came to first. His leg was broken. Karen had blood on her face but was conscious. The kids were dazed, crying, huddled in the back seat.

And from the trees… they came.

Tall, misshapen men. Mud-colored skin. Sloped foreheads. Eyes that didn't blink. They grunted and slobbered, hooting as they approached, carrying hooks, knives, cleavers.

"Time for butcherin'!" one howled, voice guttural and slurred.

Greg tried to open the door.

Then— A roar.

Not from a man. Not from a cat.

Something in-between.

The black cat stood atop the hood of the wrecked SUV, back arched, fur raised. It opened its mouth and a sound came out—something that shouldn't be possible. A blast of raw, unearthly force that shattered the windshield. The cannibals screamed and fell back.

The cat leapt

One of the hillfolk tried to grab it—his arm caught fire. Real fire. Blue flame that spread like oil across his skin. He dropped, howling, thrashing into the mud.

Another swung a blade, but the cat vanished mid-air and reappeared behind him, raking its claws across the man's throat.

No blood came out—just smoke.

Greg dragged himself from the car.

Karen got the kids out. "We have to move!"

The woods opened behind them.

The cat hissed once—this way.

They ran.

Behind them, the screams turned to shrieks of pain and terror. The hillfolk ran too—away from the cat.

PART SIX: The Edge of the Hollow

They ran. Limped, really—Greg's leg was a pulsing furnace of pain, but adrenaline pushed him on. Karen held Emma's hand tight; Noah clung to Greg's side, pale as milk. The black cat led them through the woods, weaving through trees like a phantom.

Behind them came the sounds: screams, inhuman

bellows, bones snapping, a fire crackling where no fire should be.

"What is that cat?" Karen gasped between breaths.

"I don't think it's a cat," Greg said. "Not exactly."

They followed it until the trees began to change. Slowly at first, but unmistakably—the bark lightened, the canopy thinned, and the vines gave way to wildflowers. The air was suddenly breathable again. The sky no longer looked sick.

Then, up ahead: a road.

A real road.

Paved. Painted. Sunlit.

And beyond that, in the distance—civilization.

Cell towers. Power lines.

Home.

But as they stepped toward it, the cat turned. It didn't follow.

Emma stopped and turned back. "He's not coming with us?"

The cat sat in the middle of the woods, tail curling once,

those burning green eyes fixed on her.

"He can't leave," Noah said quietly, as if understanding something no one else could.

Greg looked at the border between Burrow County and the world. It wasn't visible, not exactly—but it could be felt, like a pressure in the chest. Like stepping out of a nightmare and into the fragile skin of reality.

The cat remained still. Then it opened its mouth one last time—and from it came a sound that was not a meow, nor a roar, but something closer to a bell tolling far underground. A sound of endings.

The air shimmered. And then the cat was gone.

Vanished into the trees.

EPILOGUE: The Hollow Remembers

They made it to the nearest town, a gas station in West Virginia with an actual clerk and actual cell signal. An ambulance came. Police were called. They told their story in fragments—skipping the cat, skipping the worst of it.

Who would believe them?

The SUV was later found wrecked, torn to pieces in a ravine, far from where they'd actually escaped.

No signs of blood. No bodies. No Burrow County. On any map, there was nothing by that name. Just empty green forest.

Greg took the family home. He quit his job. Moved them to the suburbs.

They didn't go camping anymore.

They didn't drive back roads. They left the woods behind.

But Emma sometimes leaves tuna on the porch.

Noah sleeps with a flashlight under his pillow.

And Greg—some nights—wakes with a start, heart pounding, convinced he heard something soft land on the roof.

A quiet thump. A scrape of claws. A purring sound, low and comforting.

Watching.

Waiting.

Protecting.

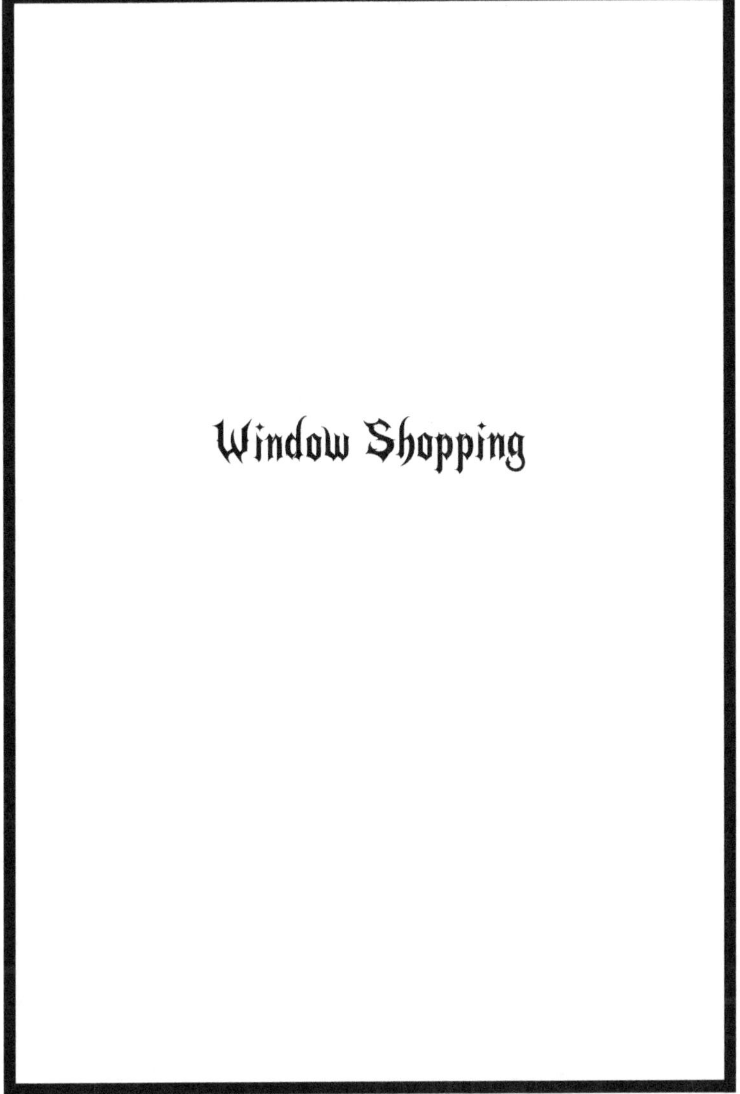

Window Shopping

The air in Ainsworth Hollow had a stillness to it that early spring afternoon, the kind that cloaked everything in the hush of something about to begin—or end. Rain hung heavy in the overcast sky, yet not a drop had fallen. The cobblestone street glistened faintly from the morning's dew, and the gas lamps, though not lit, seemed to shimmer with ghostly memory.

Eleanor Whitcombe walked alone, as she had for the last seventeen years. Her gloves were pearl grey, her parasol black lace, and her dress of deep violet velvet rustled like whispers as she moved past shuttered storefronts and faded brick façades. Her hair, the color of tarnished silver, was pinned with care beneath a veiled hat. Time had carved its name into her face, not unkindly, but with a certain dignity—a widow's grace.

She was not shopping for anything in particular. Window shopping, as her neighbor Mrs. Penworthy had once called it, was not a pursuit of things but of time. You browsed for something to fill the hour, not the cupboard. Eleanor had no real use for ribbons or French soaps or books she could no longer read without her glasses.

But the walks kept the ghosts at bay.

It was then, just as she passed the corner of Blythe & Ash Pet Emporium, that she saw it. A sleek, coal-black cat sat poised in the dusty window display between a moth-eaten dog bed and a chipped porcelain bowl.

It was not the sort of window meant to draw customers in, and yet the cat's presence transformed it into something sacred. His fur was dark as mourning silk, his eyes green as absinthe, and when he met her gaze, Eleanor felt the breath catch in her throat.

He looked directly at her, not as an animal sees a human, but as an equal sees another soul lost to time. There was no plea in his stare—only recognition. An acknowledgment of pain shared and understood. Eleanor stepped closer, gloved hand reaching toward the glass as though the barrier might melt away. A tear welled in her eye, surprising her with its suddenness.

"You poor darling," she murmured, voice nearly a whisper. "You look like you've been waiting an eternity." The cat moved, languid and graceful, walking toward the glass. He pressed his small face close, and for one strange moment, Eleanor thought she felt warmth radiate through the pane—as if he were purring not against the glass, but against her chest.

Behind her, a wind picked up, sudden and sharp, rustling the hem of her dress. The scent of lilacs, faint and oddly cloying, drifted past her nose—though no lilacs were in bloom.

"Mrs. Whitcombe?"

She turned. A familiar young man in a tweed vest, the shopkeeper, stood in the doorway with a perplexed expression. "I don't usually open until two," he said, "but if you're interested in the cat, I suppose an exception can be made."

Eleanor hesitated. She hadn't intended to adopt anything. Her house on Wraithmoor Lane was already too full of shadows. But something—perhaps the echo of an old ache, perhaps fate—moved her feet toward the door.

She followed him inside, the bell above the door chiming once, then falling silent like a coffin lid closed. The interior smelled of cedar shavings, old straw, and something darker beneath—a scent like damp stone and faded memory. "He doesn't have a name," the shopkeeper said as she approached the cage. "He was found behind the Old Chandler House three weeks ago. We thought he was feral, but he never once hissed or clawed. Just... watched. Always watching."

Eleanor knelt. The cat moved toward her fingers as if they had always belonged together. His purring began the moment she touched him, deep and resonant like the distant tremble of a funeral bell. "He reminds me of my husband," she said before she could stop herself.

The shopkeeper blinked. "I'm sorry?"

Eleanor rose, brushing her skirt. "Never mind. How much for him?"

He waved a hand. "Truth be told, I'd be relieved just to

find him a home. He's been making the other animals nervous."

By the time Eleanor left the shop, the rain had begun. Fine, cold droplets, as if the sky had finally exhaled. She held the carrier close, and the cat, nestled within, made no sound at all.

The carriage ride home was quiet, safe for the occasional groan of the wheels over uneven stones. The driver, an old man named Simms, glanced in the rearview mirror once or twice, but said nothing. Eleanor sat with the carrier in her lap, her gloved fingers tracing the brass latch as if unsure whether she had truly brought the creature home or conjured him from grief.

Her house on Wraithmoor Lane rose from the fog like a mausoleum: grey stone, ivy-choked, its upper windows long since darkened with dust and disuse. The front gate creaked open on hinges rusted from salt and time. As Simms helped her from the carriage, the cat emitted the softest mewl—not pain, not demand, but recognition.

Inside, the house was cold. Eleanor lit the hearth herself, the fire flickering uncertainly like a candle left too near the breath of something unseen. She placed the carrier before the fire and opened the door. The cat emerged slowly, his gaze sweeping the room as if he were reacquainting himself with an old haunt.

He stretched, long and lean, then leapt silently onto the arm of a velvet chaise. Eleanor watched him, struck by how he seemed to dissolve into the gloom, only his eyes retaining their vivid green fire. "You need a name," she said aloud. The clock on the mantel chimed three. She startled. She had not wound it in weeks.

The cat turned to look at her.

"Balthazar," she said suddenly, the name falling from her lips like a memory unearthed. "Yes. Balthazar."

The fire hissed as if in approval.

That night, Eleanor dreamed. She was in her old drawing room, the one they'd sealed after Arthur died. The chandelier swayed gently above her. Rain lashed the windows, though no storm could be heard. The black cat lay curled at her feet. She reached to stroke him, but his body was cold. Stiff.

Then he looked up. And Arthur's eyes stared back.

She awoke gasping, the sheets twisted about her limbs. Moonlight slanted through the window, casting the shadow of the cat across her nightgown. Balthazar sat at the foot of the bed, eyes gleaming.

Strange things followed.

The very next day, she received word that her cousin Margaret had fallen down the grand staircase at Winthrop

House—her neck broken instantly. Eleanor hadn't spoken to Margaret in years, not since the argument over Arthur's estate. Still, it felt... timely. Two days later, the glass dome over her mantel clock cracked clean down the center. No one had touched it.

Each night, Balthazar was somewhere new: on the sill of a third-floor window that hadn't opened in decades. Curled on her late husband's favorite chair, which had been mothballed in the attic. Once, she found him perched atop the mirror in her dressing room, watching her with unsettling stillness. She tried to convince herself it was coincidence. Grief. Hallucination.

Until she heard the music.

It was nearly midnight. She had descended the stairs for a cup of tea when she heard it drifting from the old music room: a waltz, her wedding waltz, played softly on the antique gramophone that hadn't worked in decades.

She opened the door slowly. Balthazar sat beside the needle arm, paw poised near the dial. He looked at her, then away, and the music stopped. That night she locked her bedroom door. And still, in the morning, he was there. Curled against her breast. Purring.

Three weeks passed.

Balthazar never left the house. He never needed to be fed—though she tried—and he never used the litter she'd bought. He simply was. A presence. A shadow.

A heartbeat in rooms that had not known warmth in years.

The neighbors began to whisper.

Old Mrs. Callahan from the rectory swore she'd seen the cat standing atop the Whitcombe mausoleum the night of the thunderstorm. "Not sitting," she told anyone who would listen, "standing upright. Like a man in mourning." Eleanor dismissed it. But the image haunted her.

Then came the second letter.

Her solicitor. Another relative—her great-nephew Alaric, whom she barely knew—had been found drowned in his own pond. No signs of struggle. Just... gone. A man in his thirties, robust, clever. A strange smile fixed to his lips when they found him. And again, Eleanor felt nothing but the distant echo of inevitability. As though these losses weren't random, but steps in a slow, spiraling dance.

One night, she confronted the cat.

She stood at the edge of the study, Balthazar curled in the crook of her husband's wingback chair. "What are you?" she asked.

He blinked.

"I should be afraid of you." The cat tilted his head, and the candle on the desk guttered. "But I'm not," she whispered. "Isn't that the strangest thing?" Silence. Then, softly, a purr. She walked to him, knelt, and touched his head. He pressed into her palm. "If you are death," she said, "then I think I've been waiting for you, too."

And somewhere behind the walls of the old house, something sighed.

Eleanor arose from her sleep. As she headed down the staircase in the morning shadows she reached for the railing, her hand missing as she stepped into nothingness that she thought was the step, she tumbled down the staircase landing at the bottom. Her tiny, elegant frame bent and broken. A few minutes later from the shadows an elegant Persian Blue cat strutted over to the body purring softly.

The cat nestled the head of the broken lady laying on the floor. She let out a loud meow. Balthazar walked over to join her. They rubbed heads as they purred and strolled into the garden to sit in their favorite spot where they enjoyed their morning tea together every morning for the last twenty years.

Salem

I. Salem

The wind moaned through the cracks in the boards of the cottage at the edge of Widdershade Hollow. The house was old—older than anyone could quite remember—and the man who lived within it, even older still. His name was Ellis Gray, and he hadn't spoken to another living soul in six weeks, save for the birds who lingered on the frostbitten branches and the trees that creaked with memory.

Ellis once had a wife and a daughter. He had once danced on spring lawns, kissed cheeks in candlelight, and laughed beneath linen skies. But time had snatched those things from him, one by one, and left him behind with brittle bones and a quiet that echoed too loud. His days were simple. Tea, books, silence. His nights—long, restless watches where the shadows moved too deliberately.

And then came Salem.

It was on a night like any other—a night of whispering trees and a moon like a cataract in the sky—when Ellis heard the scratching. Not at the door, but at the window. A low, deliberate tapping, like fingernails on glass. He shuffled over in his slippers and drew back the curtain.

There it was. A black cat. Sleek, coal-dark, eyes like winter embers. It stared straight at him through the pane, unblinking. A small shape against the storm. A shadow that didn't belong.

Ellis opened the window and it leapt in, graceful and silent as smoke. It sat on the sill and stared at him, regal and still. For a moment, Ellis just stared back.

"You're a strange one," he muttered. The cat flicked its tail. From that night on, Salem stayed.

II. Whispers in the Walls

The days grew shorter after Salem arrived. The air turned bitter, clinging to the bones like mold on old wood. Ellis didn't remember the last time he'd had company in the house, and though he told himself it was just a stray, some part of him knew that wasn't quite true. Salem wasn't like other cats.

For one thing, he never ate. Ellis had tried—he left out sardines, bits of roast, even warmed milk, but the food remained untouched. Yet the cat never appeared hungry. It simply watched, from shadowed corners or from atop the mantle, eyes wide and unnerving. Always watching.

For another, he seemed to appear in places he shouldn't. Locked doors meant nothing. Windows bolted shut in the dead of night didn't stop him from being there in the morning—curled on the bed, purring softly, his eyes glowing faintly even in the dark.

At first, Ellis tried to ignore it. After all, wasn't it nice, in a way, to have company? To wake and not feel so… abandoned?

But then came the dreams.

They started as flickers—cold forests, distant mewing, the smell of earth and ash. He saw Salem in them, always Salem, standing on the edge of something vast and terrible. And behind the cat, always just out of sight, something moved. Something old.

One night, he dreamt he was buried alive—trapped beneath soil, something purring above him. He woke clawing at his bedsheets, gasping for air. Salem sat on his chest, his eyes inches from Ellis's own.

He should have thrown the cat out. He didn't. He told himself it was the loneliness.

III. The Letter

Three weeks after Salem's arrival, Ellis received a letter.

It was odd in itself—he hadn't gotten mail in over two years. The envelope was thick, yellowed with age, the ink a faded rust. No return address. Just his name: Ellis Gray, Widdershade Hollow.

His fingers trembled as he opened it. *You are not alone. He comes with purpose. Trust the cat. Beware the hourglass.* No signature. No explanation.

He read it again, then a third time. It made no sense. When he turned to Salem, the cat was sitting on the windowsill, tail twitching. Watching him. That night, the whispering began.

At first, Ellis thought it was the wind. But the sounds were inside the walls—faint, raspy voices speaking in a language he did not understand. Salem would perk his ears, gaze at nothing, and then hiss softly, as if warding something off. By the fourth night, Ellis began sleeping with the lamp on.

IV. The Thing in the Mirror

The mirror in the upstairs hallway had belonged to his grandmother—a tall, narrow thing with carved wood and spidering cracks. Ellis had avoided it for years. Since Ruth died, he couldn't bear to look at himself for long.

But one morning, while following Salem's silent trail down the hall, he saw it. Or rather, he saw not himself. His reflection was wrong. In the glass, he stood still, but his mouth was moving. Silent. Whispering. His eyes were black pits, and behind him, in the dim light, Salem sat with two other cats—identical, dark, and watching.

He spun around. The hall was empty. When he looked back, the mirror was normal. His own face. Tired. Pale. Alone. He went to bed early that night.

But he dreamed of mirrors. Endless mirrors, each one holding a version of him more twisted than the last.

In every one, Salem watched, impassive.

V. The Buried Room

He found the door behind the cellar shelves.

It wasn't there before. Ellis would have sworn it on Ruth's grave. He'd lived in the house forty years, and there had never been a fourth wall in the basement—just stone, earth, and the smell of old coal. But Salem meowed once, sharp and loud, and pawed at the corner. The wood shelf trembled. Shifted. And behind it—rotted planks, a frame, a handle.

The door groaned when he opened it. Beyond was a room choked in dust and cobwebs. A single oil lamp burned on a crate, though no one had lit it. The walls were scrawled with symbols. Circles. Hourglasses. Eyes. In the center, a shallow depression in the dirt.

A grave. And beside it, a faded photograph. Ellis picked it up with numb fingers. It was a picture of himself. Younger. Smiling. Holding a cat. Not Salem—but close. The fur was darker. The eyes even brighter.

The back read: 1922 — Me & "Salem." He dropped it.

Because Ellis had been born in 1946.

VI. Salem Speaks

The next morning, he awoke to find Salem on his chest again. Only this time, the cat opened its mouth and spoke.

The voice was not a cat's voice. It was deep, rattling, as if formed in the lungs of a dying man. "You are marked, Ellis Gray. You were chosen long ago. The hollow remembers."

Ellis tried to move, but he couldn't. His limbs were frozen. His tongue stuck to the roof of his mouth. Salem blinked. "You buried something. Long ago. Before this life. Before this skin. It wants out." The room went black.

When he came to, he was standing in the woods behind the house. The trees loomed tall and strange, their limbs twisted into arcs. Salem sat on a stump nearby, tail curling. At his feet, a spade. And a fresh mound of earth.

VII. Beneath the Hollow

Ellis didn't remember digging. He only remembered standing over the open pit in the woods, panting, the spade loose in his trembling hands. Salem sat beside it, tail flicking. And in the grave—something wrapped in rotting cloth, old as time, its bones blackened and fused with soil.

Ellis fell to his knees. "What is this?" he whispered. Salem turned his glowing eyes toward the thing in the earth. His voice came again, low and grave: "You. Before you were *you*."

Ellis didn't understand. Couldn't. But something within him did—some memory not from this life. His fingers reached out to touch the cloth.

As he did, the wind around them stopped. The trees fell deathly silent. A pressure gripped the air like the breath of a buried god.

A sudden scream, high and distant, echoed through the woods. Ellis recoiled. "What is happening to me?" Salem stood and rubbed against his shoulder. "The seal is broken. You called me, Ellis Gray. You opened the door. Now we must close it, before what lies below remembers its name." And with that, the cat leapt into the grave— and vanished.

VIII. The Dream Below

That night, Ellis dreamed again. He walked through tunnels of bone. The walls pulsed with faint light—veins beneath skin. The air smelled of brine and fire. Far ahead, something moved—a writhing shadow with many mouths and no eyes.

Salem walked beside him.

"You buried the gate," the cat said. "You were the gate." Ellis looked at his own hands and saw they were not hands but claws. His breath steamed black. His heart did not beat. "You chose rebirth," Salem said. "A mortal shell. But it found you again. The Hollow always remembers." A door appeared ahead—huge, iron, covered in moving symbols. "You must face it now," Salem whispered. "You must remember who you were to undo what waits."

IX. The Memory of Fire

Ellis woke screaming. The fire had gone out. Ice crept along the windows. Salem was gone. For the first time in weeks, the house felt truly empty. He rose and walked the halls, calling softly, "Salem? Salem, please..." A whisper followed him from room to room. Not in words—but sounds. Breathing. Footsteps.

He paused by the hallway mirror.

His reflection was no longer his own. It was the version of him that had buried the gate—a tall figure robed in red, face painted with ash, eyes black as coals. In his hand, a staff of bone. On his shoulder, a young black cat with two tails.

The reflection smiled at him. Then it opened its mouth—and from it poured hundreds of whispering voices. Screaming. Laughing. Chanting. Ellis smashed the mirror with his cane.

X. The Second Door

That night, the door reappeared in the basement. This time, it stood open. Salem was inside. "You must come now," the cat said. "You buried the truth. You must unearth it to be free." Ellis descended into the room. The walls bled shadows. A second door had appeared on the far side—tall, carved from black wood, inscribed with a name he had long forgotten.

"Open it," Salem commanded.

Ellis reached out, and the moment his hand touched the handle, time folded. He saw everything—his past lives, each one touched by the Hollow.

He had been a warlock in the 1600s, burned in Salem— the original Salem—with a cat by his side.

He had been a gravedigger in the 1800s, burying something that whispered in his dreams. He had been a child once, in 1919, who drowned a twin to silence the voice inside him. Each time, the black cat had found him. And each time, it had saved him—from what he truly was. From what waited inside him.

XI. The Hollow Awakens

When Ellis opened the door, he expected fire. Instead, he saw the Hollow. A great cavern of bone and memory. Tendrils of thought, like roots, pulsed from the walls. And at its center—a massive hourglass. Each grain of black sand shimmered like starlight.

Salem sat beside it. "Your time is ending, Ellis Gray. You can pass in peace—or unleash it again." Ellis stared at the hourglass. His name was carved into the glass. "But what is it?" he whispered.

"A soul trap," Salem said. "Made by your first self. To hold the ancient hunger within. To silence the dark beneath Widdershade Hollow. It has cracked."

Ellis saw the fracture—hairline thin, leaking light. "What do I do?"

"You must give your name. Your whole name. Seal the Hollow. And then I will take you."

Ellis looked down. His hands were fading."I don't remember my name."

Salem placed a paw over his chest. "I do."

And he whispered it.

XII. The Sealing

As Salem spoke the name, the cavern groaned. The hourglass cracked wider. Ellis cried out as memories poured into him—names, spells, blood rites, deaths, sacrifices, sins. All his. All lives he had tried to forget. He stepped forward and pressed his palm to the glass.

"I am the gate," he whispered. "And I shut myself." The hourglass exploded.

Light and darkness poured out and then—folded inward. A roar louder than the world itself swallowed the cavern. And in that moment, Ellis felt peace. He fell.

And Salem caught him.

XIII. The Cottage, Again

Ellis woke in his bed. The fire was burning. The windows were whole. The house was warm. And Salem sat on his chest, purring. "What… happened?"

The cat blinked slowly. "You sealed it. You chose peace. You saved yourself."

"I don't remember it all," Ellis said.

"You don't need to."

Ellis reached up and stroked Salem's fur. "Will you stay?"

"I always do. Until it's safe."

For the first time in years, Ellis wept. Not from fear. But release. Outside, the trees no longer whispered. The Hollow had gone silent.

XIV. The Final Day

Ellis lived three more months. They were his best months—quiet, full of tea and books and sunshine on the porch. Salem stayed by his side, curling beside him each night. When the end came, it came gently. Ellis closed his eyes on a warm spring afternoon, with Salem curled against his chest. His final breath was a sigh of thanks.

Epilogue: The New Door

Years later, the house sat empty again. Until a stormy night, when a young woman running from something she would not name stumbled into Widdershade Hollow.

She found the door ajar. And a black cat waiting by the fire.

Its eyes glowed faintly.

It meowed once. And the Hollow remembered her name.

Hanna

The Meadow's Watcher

On a cold fall night, the moon cast a pallid glow over the remains of an old stone house. Its crumbling chimney jutted out from the tangled ivy like the spine of some ancient beast, long dead and half-forgotten. The surrounding meadow was silent, a great swath of silvered grass stretching under the gaze of the night sky. Nothing stirred, save for a lone shadow moving with purpose.

It was a cat—a small, muscular tabby, its fur striped like smoke and ash. Its eyes, two glistening emeralds, caught every trick of the light. The cat did not move like a creature of flesh and bone. No, it glided—silently, preternaturally—across the field. It paused at the foot of the ruin, its tail flicking once. Far off down the lane, under a withered elm, headlights pierced the fog.

The car rolled slowly, tires crunching gravel, until it stopped in front of a rusted gate that hung askew. The driver stepped out, flashlight in hand, and swung the beam over the old sign hammered into a fence post: Millcreek Farm – Est. 1804.

Henry Alder had never believed in signs or omens. A practical man in his late fifties, he had come to the countryside for solitude, for a reprieve from the chaos that had, in the city, become unbearable.

It was supposed to be temporary—just a few months, a season or two. Just long enough to quiet the noise in his head. He didn't notice the cat watching him.

The house he rented was modest, one of the few habitable structures left in the village outskirts. Though worn, its bones were good—oak beams, leaded glass, a working hearth. The kind of place meant to outlast its occupants. It suited Henry just fine.

The next morning, when he opened the front door to retrieve the newspaper (though the nearest town was five miles off and hardly current), he found the cat sitting on the steps. Its green eyes locked with his, unblinking. "Where'd you come from?" he muttered.

The cat meowed once—low, but clear.

Despite himself, Henry opened the door wider. With certainty.

Henry didn't consider himself a pet person. In truth, he had always found animals slightly unpredictable—too expressive in their silence. But there was something about the cat's eyes that morning. Something almost… human. It padded into the house without hesitation, tail aloft like a banner, and proceeded to make itself at home, curling on the tattered rug before the hearth as if it had always lived there.

He called it Ash, for its color and for the soot it seemed to trail wherever it went, though he never saw it roll in the fireplace or creep through grime. He didn't mean to keep it. But he never made any real attempt to put it out.

It stayed. Strange things began to happen.

It started subtly—small things. Henry would leave the kettle on the stove and come back to find it already boiling. Lights flickered not in the typical way old bulbs do, but as if in response to his movement. He chalked it up to rural electricity, damp air, bad wiring. But then the sounds started.

Voices—low murmurs in the walls, too faint to understand. They crept in during twilight, between the turning of the wind and the fall of night. At first, he assumed it was the creak of old beams settling, the rustle of mice in the insulation. But the whispers grew more deliberate. He could hear names. His name. Henry. Whispered like a prayer. Or a warning.

The cat would always appear when the sounds began, leaping soundlessly to the sill and staring out into the dark with those impossible green eyes, as though watching something Henry could not see. Something that watched back.

About two weeks after Ash arrived, Henry decided to explore the meadow. It was late afternoon, fog clinging to the earth like a second skin, the air tinged with the smell of fallen leaves and earth turned cold. The old stone house at the far end loomed like a broken tooth in a dying jaw.

Ash followed.

The cat moved ahead, weaving through the grasses, its path unwavering. Henry hesitated at the edge of the rubble, half-buried under time and rot. The ruin pulsed with a sort of unspoken menace, though there was no wind and no sound but the ticking of unseen insects. Still, he stepped closer.

A rusted iron stove lay in pieces beside a collapsed hearth. Part of the flooring remained, warped and blackened by time, though it hinted at the elegant structure it once was. Something about the layout struck Henry as familiar—but he'd never been here before, had he?

Ash let out a strange noise—somewhere between a hiss and a moan—and leapt up onto what remained of a stone windowsill. Its body went rigid.

Henry felt it too. The air around him shifted. It grew heavy, like invisible hands pressing into his skin. The silence was no longer just absence of sound. It was a thing, alive and watching. He turned back. He did not return to the ruin again. Not for a while.

By the third week, Henry could no longer ignore the dreams. They came nightly and always began the same way: he stood at the foot of the old stone house, moonlight scalding the grass around him white. The windows flickered with dim candlelight, though the house had no roof and barely any walls.

He'd hear laughter—children's laughter, joyous and shrill—and a woman humming a tune just beyond recognition. But when he stepped inside, it would all fall silent.

And something would breathe behind him. Each time, he woke gasping, cold sweat clinging to his chest. And each time, the cat would be curled on his chest, purring softly, as though anchoring him to this world.

He began to read local histories. The village library was little more than a converted barn, but the records went back centuries. Millcreek Farm had belonged to the Weatherall family, once prominent landowners.

The matriarch, Lavinia Weatherall, had lived there with her children during the late 1800s. But something had happened—some great fire. The house burned. None of them were ever found.

Locals whispered that Lavinia was a witch, that her soul had been bound to the land through blood rites and ancient oaths. That the cat—a strange, ever-returning tabby with green eyes—was her familiar, cursed to linger, waiting. Waiting for what?

Ash grew more possessive. It no longer tolerated guests—on the rare occasions Henry drove into town and brought back someone from the diner or the store, the cat would hiss, arch its back, and stare with unblinking disdain until the person left.

Odd smells would linger in the air—burnt sage, copper, wet earth.

His neighbors—what few there were—began to treat him differently. Their eyes lingered too long. They crossed the street when they saw him approach. And the children had taken to chanting songs when they saw him:

> Green eyes in the dark,
> She'll scratch out your heart.
> Cross the field and you will see
> She's not a cat—she's the key.

Henry began to see shapes in the corner of his vision. Figures dressed in soot-black robes. A woman with hair like smoke and eyes like fire, standing just beyond the windows when he passed. But when he turned, she was never there.

Only the cat. Always the cat.

It happened in early December. A snow had fallen—not heavy, but enough to muffle the landscape in silence. Henry had just returned from town, where the shopkeeper refused to meet his eyes, and the radio in his car stuttered with strange static that pulsed in rhythm with his heartbeat.

Ash sat in the window, tail flicking with strange agitation. As Henry approached the door, he noticed something carved into the frame—fine and shallow, as if etched by claws or a knife: "We Remember."

That night, the dreams changed.

He stood once more at the ruined house, but this time, it was whole. Firelight flickered from within. He could smell roasted meat, hear the low murmur of voices. Someone was weeping. The front door stood ajar. He stepped through. Inside, time had folded like paper. A Victorian parlor stood as pristine as it might have been a century ago.

A long table stretched across the room, set for supper. At the head sat Lavinia Weatherall. Her hair was pinned in coils, her black gown shimmering with age and dust. Her skin, though pale, was flawless. She raised her gaze to Henry—and smiled.

"You've done well to return," she said. "I don't understand," Henry whispered. "You were here before," she replied. "Long before. You made a promise." The cat sat at her feet. And then the world dissolved. He woke screaming. Ash was standing on his chest, claws extended just slightly into his skin, eyes glowing like twin lanterns. In that moment, Henry remembered.

Not in flashes—but all at once.

A century ago, he had lived on this land. His name had been Elias Weatherall, Lavinia's brother. He had watched her descent into grief and madness after her children perished from a fever that took them all in one week.

She had begged him to help bring them back. She'd found old rites, ancient things buried in half-translated books.

He had agreed. And they had summoned something. Not the children, but something that wore their faces.

Something that took the warmth of the house and never gave it back. Lavinia had tried to bind it. To stop it. She'd sacrificed herself, tethering her soul—and the creature's—to the land.

Elias had fled. Coward that he was. And now, a hundred years later, the land had called him home. Not as punishment. As penance. His soul had found its way back into a new body. A new name. But the same debt.

Ash had come to collect. From that night forward, Henry changed. He no longer avoided the ruin. In fact, he began walking to it daily, always with Ash at his side. The meadow seemed to respond—ferns curled back, the air stilled. The ruin felt less threatening now, almost reverent. Inside the hearth's remains, Henry found something new—a ring, untouched by rust, resting among the stones. It bore the Weatherall crest. When he slipped it on, he felt a pulse up his arm and saw, just for a moment, the house as it had been.

Each night, Henry grew weaker. Not ill—but faded. Like something inside him was draining, migrating elsewhere.

He lost time. Woke in strange places—once in the field, barefoot, fingers covered in ash.

Another time, kneeling before the hearth in his own house, whispering in a language he didn't know.

Ash remained close. Always watching. Never speaking—but always listening. One morning, he woke and knew. He dressed in his warmest coat and walked out across the meadow for the last time. Snowflakes drifted in lazy spirals, vanishing before they touched the ground. The sky had taken on a strange color—neither dusk nor dawn, but something in-between. Ash led the way. At the stone house, the ruins shimmered. The air wavered like heat rising from summer roads. And then it changed.

The house stood whole again. Lavinia waited at the door. "You have come back," she said.

"I am ready," Henry—*Elias*—replied.

Inside, the table was set again. A great black tome lay open in the center. The words burned in gold. The ritual began—not of summoning, but of release. Ash leapt to the table, crouched above the book, and let out a long, keening cry. The air split.

The thing that had once been bound beneath the land stirred.

A great sigh of ancient hunger, of pain and memory and

not meant for words. The room grew dark—but Henry stepped forward. I give myself," he said. "Let them go."

The light around him flared. Lavinia began to weep—not from sorrow, but from gratitude. The creature recoiled, writhing as the circle pulsed with fire.

Then—Silence.

Henry died in his sleep that night. No pain. No struggle. Simply a quiet exhale, and then nothing. When his body was found weeks later, curled in his bed as though simply napping, Ash was gone. No pawprints in the snow. No scent, no sound. But had someone been there, they would have seen, just before the final breath left him, a shimmer pass over Henry's eyes. And standing at the foot of the bed, the cat. Its green eyes glowed, and then—

A door opened. And Henry rose. He turned to Ash, and the cat turned, leading him into a place where the world dimmed and the stars sang. Not heaven. Not hell. But the truth beneath it all.

A place where debts are paid and souls are made whole.

ABOUT THE AUTHOR

David Ray Foster's life story is a compelling testament to resilience and determination. Born in a poor holler in Charleston, West Virginia, David faced severe hardships from an early age. He was placed in an orphanage at the age of ten, and by fifteen he was living on the streets as a runaway.

Despite these daunting challenges, he earned his GED and soon thereafter was recruited to be an undercover narcotics agent, which started his life-long career in law enforcement.

Alongside his work, David pursued higher education with a focus on criminal justice at Metropolitan Community College in Kansas City, Missouri. He further broadened his knowledge by studying psychology and religion at St. Leo University in Florida.

He authored many police training books and policy manuals, demonstrating his ability to communicate complex ideas clearly and effectively. These writing endeavors not only enhanced police practices but also refined his own skills as an author. After a dedicated career, he retired from police work in 2018.

David has two grown daughters, and currently resides in St. Joseph, Missouri, where he shares his home with several mysterious felines who have inspired these stories.

Other Titles from Strange Moon Press LLC

<u>Available Now</u>

A Monstrous Feast by Phoebe Buskey
ISBN 979-8-218-61935-0

Help Wanted, Inquire Within (anthology)
ISBN 979-8-218-79920-5

Stories from Sunnyside Cemetery (anthology)
ISBN 979-8-9936917-0-1

Psychic Gambles by Aleks Stajkovic Jr.
ISBN 979-8-9936917-1-8

<u>Coming Soon</u>

The Mirror by David Rincon (fantasy)

The Collected Works of Dark Lorecraft (speculative mythology)

Little Green Men (anthology)